LOVE IS A BATTERFIELD

RAISED AND GLAZED COZY MYSTERIES, BOOK 8

EMMA AINSELY

SUMMER PRESCOTT BOOKS PUBLISHING

CHAPTER ONE

Maggie Sharpe stood over the baker's table in the kitchen of her donut shop and stared at the dough in front of her. She placed one hand on her hip and the other on the table to steady herself. "I don't know what I've done," she said, turning to her best friend and business partner, Ruby Cobb.

"Let me take a look." Ruby dried her hands off on a towel and tossed it on the prep table. As a former executive chef, she was the go-to authority when anything appeared off or went wrong. Mostly, though, Maggie had things well in hand.

Except for this morning, of course.

"Where did you get the yeast?" Ruby asked her after probing the dough for a second.

"The storeroom." Maggie gestured behind her. "It was the newest based on the last shipment we had."

"Hold on," Ruby said. She picked up the packaging from the trash can and headed to the storeroom. Maggie followed. "These are all out-of-date. Every last one of them." She handed the nearest package to Maggie and pointed out the date.

"These expired three months ago!" Maggie gasped.

"Gather all of these up and I'll call the warehouse," Ruby said. "I'll let Myra know, too, so she can let all the customers know what's going on." Another perk of her former life as a chef was her ability to navigate the tangled lines of restaurant supply shipping and delivery.

"And I will plan today's menu around cake donuts instead of anything yeast-based." Maggie returned to the table and scooped the entire mess of dough into the tall trash can next to the table. She slapped the flour off of her hands and brushed them down the front of her apron.

"I have an idea," Myra Sawyer said a few minutes later as she emerged from the front of the donut shop with a tray of sugar canisters to refill before the doors opened for the morning.

"What's your idea?" Maggie asked her young employee.

"Let's serve mini donuts today with the rest of them," she said. "Just run home and drive the food truck here and we can run all of the machines at once."

"That's sort of brilliant," Ruby said from the office.

"I think you're right." Maggie untied her apron and tossed it on the baker's table. "Be right back." She grabbed her keys and jacket and headed out the door.

Fifteen minutes later, Maggie returned with the food truck. She parked it in the alley behind the shop, close enough that she could pull the long electrical connection from the housing on the side of the truck and connect it to the outlet in the back of her building.

A little while later, Maggie returned to the larger kitchen and announced that the mini donut machine was up and running. "I'm going to run it solidly for the next two hours," she said. "We'll sack them up by the dozens, and I've also got the other fryer going for the chocolate glazed minis."

"I'll come out in about an hour to relieve you," Orson Hawley announced after arriving for his shift. He stood just inside the kitchen door and tied his apron around his thin waist. For a man in his late sixties, he could run around the kitchen with the youngest of them. He was also known for his curmudgeonly outlook on life, and beloved for it.

"You want to run the food truck?" Maggie asked. "I can take care of it, Orson."

"Maybe I would like a chance to run the show out there myself," he said. "I'm not sure if I'll ever get to run the food truck alone, and this is close enough to home base that I actually can."

Ruby winked at Maggie from the other side of the kitchen. Orson had little reservation in sharing what he thought, and in this case, they both appreciated his candor. Since he was hired at the donut shop, he took every opportunity to learn or try new things, even to the point of inventing new menu selections and suggesting ideas to Maggie and Ruby.

"Alright, then," Maggie said. "You just come right on out when you're ready to take over."

Orson saluted smartly and went out to the dining room. She gathered up a basket filled with supplies from the storeroom and headed back out into the parking lot.

True to his word, an hour later, Orson opened the large back door and joined her inside the food truck. "Show me what you've got going on and then leave me to it," he ordered.

Maggie walked him through the running of the automatic donut machine and the plans she had for the mini fryer. She left him with instructions on quantities and headed back inside.

"Maybe the bad yeast was a blessing in disguise," she said to Ruby after the first morning rush died down. The mini donut offerings had sold so fast that Myra and Ruby had each taken a turn at running the truck out back, too.

"Yeah, it sort of makes me wonder about parking the truck here a couple of times each week," Ruby said. "If we did it every day the novelty might wear off, but a couple of times during the week would be pretty lucrative, I think."

Maggie considered the possibility. She thought for a solid minute before she spoke again. "I think that's an excellent idea. And you know what else? Baseball and then football season will be here before we know it. We should check into parking the truck at the high school during home games."

"Myra should head that up," Ruby suggested.

"Oh, yes, she should."

"Myra needs to do what?" she asked when she joined them from the front of the donut shop.

"You need to look into running the food truck at home high school baseball and football games this year," Maggie answered.

"And possibly once or twice each week right here in the parking lot," Ruby added.

"You're going to run that contraption out here in the parking lot?" Orson asked when he emerged from the cooler.

"That's one idea," Maggie said. "I'm sensing you don't think it's a good one?"

Orson's eyes widened. "On the contrary. I think it's an excellent idea, but I was going to say that weekends and Wednesday nights might be the best times. Catch the churchgoing crowd before and after their meetings."

"Maybe you should head this project up," Myra said with a wink. "Sounds like you're the one almost done with the college education in business management, and not me."

"Oh, you go on," Orson said, and then promptly blushed from all of the attention. Myra smiled and headed back through the two-way swinging door that separated the kitchen from the front dining area.

Maggie returned to drying the dishes she had washed up from the food truck while Ruby put the finishing touches on the daily lunch special. Orson positioned himself on a stool and sipped his latest cup of coffee.

"I propose the next major purchase we make for the donut shop be an industrial dishwasher," Maggie said. She smoothed lotion over her hands and waved them in the air. "I'm sick of my hands feeling like I've been skinning fish in Alaska in the middle of January."

"You wouldn't be skinning fish in Alaska in January," Orson said. Ruby shot Maggie a knowing look. In addition to his sunny demeanor, Orson was infamous for his self-proclaimed knowledge of just about everything.

Maggie was about to ask him what he meant when Myra returned with another wide smile on her face. "Maggie, there's a man here to see you."

"There is? Who is it?" She wiped her hands down the front of her apron.

"As if we don't already know," Orson muttered. "I bet he's wearing a blue uniform and driving a white car with "Dogwood Mountain Police Department' written down the side."

Still grinning, Myra shook her head. "No, this isn't Chief Mission. This one is much younger, blond, and about as tall as a tree."

"It can't be."

"It can't be what?" Orson asked.

Maggie didn't wait around to answer him. She headed straight for the swinging door and didn't stop. Orson, Ruby, and Myra filed in behind her.

When she reached the other side, Maggie froze, dead in her tracks. There, standing in front of her, was the one face on the planet she would never have expected to see staring back at her.

"My goodness," she said softly. "It really is you."

The young man stepped beyond the counter and spread his arms open wide in front of Maggie. "Mom," he said, and then pulled her into a strong embrace.

CHAPTER TWO

"Everyone, this is my son, Ensign Bradley Sharpe," Maggie said, still floating a foot off of the ground after seeing the face of her only child in the middle of her donut shop. "Bradley, meet Myra Sawyer, Orson Hawley, and Ruby Cobb."

Bradley stepped forward first to Ruby and pulled her into a tight hug. "My mother tells me that you are the closest thing to a living aunt I have," he said. "It's very good to meet you."

"That's high praise, coming from your mom, Bradley." Ruby returned his embrace and then wiped a tear from her eye. "I can't tell you how much we have heard about you, young man."

"All good things, I hope." He moved to Orson and extended his hand. "Mr. Hawley, it is a pleasure to meet you as well."

Orson stood taller than they had ever seen him stand before. "Young man, the pleasure is all mine. We're all very proud of you and your service to this country."

Ruby smiled at Maggie. Never before had they seen the old man so authentically impressed with another human being.

"I'm Myra. I work here with your mom and these other guys," Myra said next. "I'm proud to meet you as well. It helps me understand why your mom is so willing to give people like me a chance." Despite how young she was, she'd lived a life that most others couldn't imagine.

Bradley took her hand. "My mother has expressed her gratitude for you in her letters many times over, Myra," he said. "I'm quite certain you have repaid any favors she has given you long before now."

Bradley turned back to his mother. "What are you doing here?" she asked him. "Not that I'm not over the moon excited to see you. I'm just shocked that you're here, in the flesh, standing right in front of me."

"I had a chance at a thirty-day shore leave, and I didn't let the dust settle on me before I took it," Bradley said. "I came here because I wanted to see about this new home you've created for yourself. I wanted to see what renewed your lease on life, Mom."

Maggie pulled him into a tight hug once again. "I just can't believe my eyes." Tears streamed down her face as she spoke. "I just can't believe it."

"Maggie, is everything okay?" She looked up to see Brett standing right behind her son. "Are you alright?" He eyed Bradley carefully.

"Oh, Brett," Maggie said. "I'm better than I have been in years. I'd like you to meet my son, Bradley. He is an Ensign in the Navy. Honey, this is my… well, this is my boyfriend and our local chief of police, Brett Mission."

The men exchanged handshakes. Bradley turned back to his mom. "Is this the same guy you went to high school with?"

"The very one," Maggie said, thankful no one had made a huge deal about her use of the word boyfriend. Being in her forties, it felt a bit awkward to call him that, but it was the truth.

"It's nice to meet you, sir," Bradley said.

"Are you here on shore leave?" Brett asked him.

"Thirty days," Bradley answered. "Did you serve, sir?"

Brett nodded. "I did. But in the army," he said. "It's nice that you're here to see your mama, son." With that, he turned and headed for the restroom on the other side of the donut shop.

A question passed through Maggie's mind, but she dismissed it. As soon as Brett made his way to the other side of the dining room, the door opened, and a tall redhead dressed in high heels and a short pencil skirt made her way in. She walked straight for Bradley and twisted her arm through his as soon as she reached him. "What's taking so long, sweetheart?" she said quietly.

"Sweetheart?" Maggie asked. She noticed the front of the woman's shirt for the first time and the large, protruding belly it covered. The woman was very pregnant and still very attached to her son.

"Mom, everyone, I would like for you to meet my wife, Cynthia Sharpe," Bradley said.

"Cynthia Boone Sharpe," the woman corrected. She reached her hand out and gripped Ruby's on her own. "I suppose this makes you my mom, too."

Ruby carefully peeled Cynthia's hand off of her own. "I have no offspring," she said. "I think you meant this one." She pulled her hand toward Maggie and then dropped it.

"Oh, I am so ashamed of myself! I should have seen it right away," Cynthia said. "You have the same eyes as Bradley!"

Maggie regained her composure and took the woman's hand more fully in her own. "I don't mean to sound presumptuous, but am I to assume…"

"That we're a family?" Cynthia asked. She ran her hand over her rounded belly and gushed. "You assume right!"

"Mom, this is my wife Cynthia." Bradley beamed. "And as you can already see, we are about to have a family."

Maggie accepted a hug from Cynthia, and an even longer embrace from her son. "I have so many questions. Like, how long are you here? Are you staying somewhere in town?"

"We're here for a couple of days," Cynthia answered. "We came in last night and Bradley wanted to surprise you."

"We're staying at the Dogwood House," Bradley added. "I thought it would be cool to see the house you spent so much time in when you were growing up."

"You are welcome to stay with me," Maggie said. "I have an extra bedroom."

Bradley shook his head. "Thanks, Mom," he said. "But this is sort of a last-minute babymoon for us. We're already checked in and settled there."

"What is a babymoon?" Myra asked.

"It's sort of like a honeymoon, but you take it before the baby comes and you can't get away again for a while," Cynthia said.

"Oh, I get it," Myra said. "That sounds awesome."

"Where are you headed after this?" Maggie asked.

"New Orleans," Bradley said. "We want to be there for about a week."

Maggie had more questions than she could think of. What she wanted to do more than anything was take her son aside and ask him a zillion things, starting with when and where he met the woman who was now his wife.

"Well, I can't get over what a surprise this is," Maggie said at last. "I have to hang around here for a little while and then I would love to spend some more time with you both."

Brett reappeared behind them. He waved slightly at her and then headed for the door without ordering his usual cinnamon roll and cinnamon latte. Maggie distractedly waved back.

"We can handle things around here," Ruby interjected. "Why don't you go on and spend some time with your son? And later tonight, if you're all up for it, I would love to have you all over for a bonfire and barbecue at the farm."

"Oh, Ruby, you don't have to do that," Maggie said.

"I don't know, Mom, barbecue?" Bradley grinned. The rest of them laughed and Ruby placed her hand on his arm.

"You forget, Auntie Ruby is a former chef," she teased. "When I say barbecue, I am not talking about hotdogs and hamburgers."

"Deal," Bradley said. He hugged her again with his arm around her shoulders and then turned back to his mother. "Give us an hour or so and we'll stop by the cottage to see you. My phone battery is about to die, so take down Cynthia's number just in case." He rattled off the number and she programmed it into her phone.

"Deal." Maggie grinned. "I can't wait!"

CHAPTER THREE

That evening, the fire blazed in the middle of a circle of outdoor chairs. Maggie gave up her favorite Adirondack chair for her new daughter-in-law, although the fact hadn't quite hit her yet that she actually had a new daughter-in-law.

Her son was in Dogwood Mountain, sitting in front of her with his dinner including Ruby's jalapeño marinated steak sandwiches and gourmet baked beans. Maggie's contribution of grilled spiced pears with homemade vanilla ice cream would round out the meal. Everything seemed so normal, yet so very strange.

"So, when are we going to hear the story?" Myra asked. She sat in a camping chair next to Brooks

Macklin, a recent addition to the Dogwood Mountain Police Department and her special friend.

"What story?" Bradley asked. "Oh, how we met?"

"That would be the story, Squid," Brooks added with a grin.

"Squid? You must be the neighborhood jarhead," Bradley replied.

"Former Marine here." Brooks reached across Cynthia, who was seated to his right and gripped Bradley's hand in his own. "Semper Fi, buddy."

"Always faithful." Bradley smiled.

Brooks turned to Myra. "How do you like being surrounded by old military guys like us?" he asked.

"Like either of you are very old." Myra scoffed.

"Chief Mission was in the military, too," Brooks said. "And he's old."

The comment brought a group-wide "whoop" from everyone. "You do realize that Chief Mission is younger than a couple of us here," Ruby said. She glanced at Orson. "In some cases, significantly younger."

Cynthia stood up then and turned her attention to Ruby. "I'm afraid nature is calling," she said. "Where did you say the restroom is?"

"I'll show you." Ruby led the pregnant woman toward the house.

"So, tell us." Myra turned back to Bradley. "Where did you meet Cynthia?"

"She is the sister of one of my bunkmates, Cal Boone. I'm sure I've told you some stories about him before." He looked at his mother. "His family and close friends had flown in from the States to see him in Japan. I was on a holiday as well and we all met for dinner."

"I can't believe that you got married and you didn't tell me," Maggie said. She tossed a wadded napkin at her son for emphasis.

"It didn't happen until a month ago, Mom," he said. "By then, I knew that I wanted to tell you in person."

"Were you engaged for a long time?" Myra persisted in her questions, and Maggie was grateful that she was asking the things she most wanted to know. It was easier to come from someone besides his mother.

Bradley shook his head and blushed slightly. "Not at all," he said. "I hadn't heard from her for months. I mean, we really hit it off in Japan, if you couldn't tell. But after that weekend, we had no further contact."

"Son, are you telling me that your wife didn't bother to tell you that she was carrying your child until just a little while ago?" Orson asked. His question came without the typical acidity in his tone.

"Orson," Maggie said quietly.

"I'm just concerned," he said. "I know how these things can go."

"It's okay, Mom," Bradley said. "His question is legit."

"It is most definitely not okay," Cynthia snapped. "I'm not sure where you'd get an idea like that about me, but it's best never to put it into your mouth again."

"Cynthia," Bradley chastised. "That's my mother and her friends you are talking to."

"Oh, I know that," Cynthia said. She brightened her demeanor and smiled. "I was just saying that for future reference."

Maggie forced a smile through clenched teeth. The reason they'd get an idea like that is because they didn't know the woman from a hole in ground. But she kept her mouth shut, not wanting to cause a scene.

"We were talking about how the two of you met," Myra offered. Her comment seemed to cut through the tension that was building. "Bradley said that you ran into each other in Japan. I've always wanted to visit Tokyo."

"Bradley and my brother are friends," she said. "We met when my parents and I flew there to see him."

Maggie sat back for a moment. She didn't want to think the thoughts in her head, but there was something that just felt off about the woman holding her son's hand and the situation that brought them together. She continued to listen, trying hard to smile and nod every now and then to show she was paying attention. And she was, but everything felt too surreal to compute. She needed more time to process.

CHAPTER FOUR

At nine, Maggie rose to help Ruby get dessert. She checked the ice cream maker and spooned out the vanilla concoction. Myra had volunteered to grill the cut pears on the outside grill while Maggie prepared the syrup on the stove inside.

"You are swimming around in an ocean of thoughts, aren't you?" Ruby asked her.

"You have no idea," Maggie replied absentmindedly.

"Well, I think it's very understandable that you are a little bit overwhelmed," Ruby continued. "First, your only child appears out of nowhere, which is wonderful for sure, but he brings along with him a woman you've never met and introduces her as his wife, and she is visibly very pregnant. That's a lot."

Maggie stared at the liquid swirling in the pan. "I am utterly speechless," she said. "I'm trying to separate the shock from my true impressions of Cynthia."

"That's not an unusual reaction. She is a little much to take in." Ruby leaned close to Maggie and kept her voice low. "Let alone the shock that you are about to become a grandmother."

Maggie dropped the spoon into the saucepan. She gazed up at the ceiling. "Oh, my gosh," she said. "I don't know why that hasn't registered to me yet. I'm going to be a grandma."

"Yes, you are." Ruby smiled and draped her arm around Maggie's shoulders. "This is a happy thing."

"Oh, I know that! I just can't believe it." Maggie wiped a tear as it rolled down her cheek. "Since Aunt Marjorie died and Bradley's dad and I divorced, my family has been so disconnected. But now, this happens."

"Maybe focus on that right now, and not the other parts of all of this," Ruby suggested. "I know that's going to be hard, but I think in the long run that's the best way to look at this."

Maggie smiled, stood up taller, and turned off the stove. "The sauce is ready," she said. Her mood had brightened considerably already.

"Perfect. And here I thought I was the chef." Ruby winked and gave Maggie a playful nudge.

"I think these pears are ready," Myra said through the door.

Ruby handed Maggie a dish to pour the sauce in and pulled the ice cream from the freezer. "Let's go have some dessert."

Maggie held the door open for her friend and whispered, "thank you" as she passed.

"Come on, Mimi," Ruby replied.

"Mimi?"

"Yeah, I like that better than just plain 'grandma.'"

Maggie shut the door behind her and headed for Ruby's outdoor kitchen area. She opened the lid to her smaller grill and began to remove the hot pears and place each one in a bowl. Ruby added a scoop of homemade ice cream on top and then drizzled the syrup over it.

"Bradley," Maggie called out. "Would you like to come and get some for yourself and the mother-to-be?"

"Oh, I love ice cream," Cynthia said. She grabbed the bowl eagerly when Bradley handed it to her. She spooned a bite into her mouth and closed her eyes. "This is so good. Thank you."

"You're welcome, Cynthia." Maggie felt her heart swell. "And if you and that grandbaby of mine decide that you want more, you just let me know."

"I will." Cynthia smiled. Bradley sat down next to her and gripped her hand.

"This is fabulous, Mom," he said between mouthfuls.

Ruby passed out more bowls. Myra accepted a bowl and then passed one to Brooks. "Hang on a second," he said. He pointed toward the road. A pair of head-lights turned into the driveway. Maggie immediately recognized the police chief's car. He'd said he was unable to come to Ruby's because he had to work late, but she was glad he'd found the time.

"Is something wrong?" Ruby asked, seeing the look on Brook's face.

Brooks shrugged. "I don't know. The chief just texted me and asked me to meet him in the driveway."

"Well, invite him to come and sit by the fire and enjoy something he has likely never tasted before," Ruby said.

Brooks gave her a thumbs up and headed for the driveway. Brett stood in the open car door. He waved distractedly at the group. Maggie tried not to stare, but the look on his face told her there was something wrong.

She felt her stomach flip, and not in a good way.

Brooks stood with his back to the house for several moments. Maggie and the rest of the group ate quietly while the two police officers conferred. After a minute, Brooks turned around and looked at them. He gestured a couple of times. Brett nodded his head and frowned, and then gestured himself toward the group.

Maggie could almost hear him telling the younger officer: "Let's get on with it."

Brett left his car running as he walked slowly toward the group. Maggie noticed that, while he wore street clothes, his gun was attached to his hip.

"What's going on, Chief?" Orson asked before Brett had the chance to speak.

"I'm afraid that I need to have a word with Ensign Sharpe," he said.

Maggie knew the look on his face well enough to stand up and drop her plate. "What is it, Brett? What's the matter, and why do you need to speak with my son?" she asked.

Brett raised his hand and gently patted the air. "It's just something I need to discuss with him," he said. "I'm sorry, but this needs to be between Bradley and me."

Bradley stood up then and nodded. "Let's go over there then, Chief."

"Wait, what's going on here?" Cynthia asked. She pulled at Bradley's hand and refused to let go. "I am his wife, and I need you to tell me what is happening."

"Let go, honey," Bradley said. With his free hand, he peeled her hand off of his. "I'll be right back. I'm sure that everything is fine."

Maggie barely noticed her new daughter-in-law's behavior. She watched her son intently as he walked toward the police car with Brett. All at once, he stopped in his tracks and faced Brett. In the firelight, she could see that the color had drained from his face.

"Oh, no," she breathed. In her mind, she knew it was news about his father, her ex-husband. Something had happened to him, so they informed Bradley. Of course, they would inform his son. She was no longer his wife, after all.

How would they know he was there? Because he would have informed the Navy where he would be. They would contact local law enforcement to let him know what happened. These thoughts crowded her head in the moments it took for the two men to approach the police cruiser. Maggie sighed once, slightly relieved.

Her relief was short-lived. She heard the unfamiliar cry of her daughter-in-law when Brett turned her son around and ordered him to put his hands behind his back. Maggie's shouts joined Cynthia's when Brett

CHAPTER FIVE

The world around her spun. Maggie felt a burning sensation in her throat. It didn't occur to her that the burning was tightness from the anxiety attack she was suffering. She reached out for something to hold on to as her legs weakened under her.

She felt a strong hand on her shoulder and looked up into the face of her new friend, Brooks. "Maggie," he was saying. "Let's go inside so we can talk. I need you to help me with Cynthia."

Cynthia. Cynthia and the baby. Maggie was instantly calmed. She nodded her head soberly. Her throat ached. Someone shoved a glass of water into her hand. She barely registered Ruby's face in her mind.

They walked into the kitchen. It wasn't her kitchen, nor was it the donut shop kitchen. The farmhouse, she was at Ruby's farm. Her thoughts unscrambled a bit. "Brooks," she said. "Why was he taken away? What is going on?"

"Just a minute and I'll tell you," Brooks said. "In the meantime, we need to calm Cynthia down."

Maggie walked further into the house. She found Myra kneeling on the floor in front of the kitchen table. Cynthia's hand was in her own.

"I think we need to call an ambulance," Myra looked up and said.

Maggie's eyes focused on Cynthia. She sat hunched forward gasping for air. Before she could think another thought, she was at her side.

"Cynthia, try to calm down," she said. "You need to be calmer for the baby."

"She's hyperventilating," Brooks said. "I've called for an ambulance."

A moment later, two paramedics entered the house pushing a gurney in front of them. In short order,

Cynthia was loaded onto the gurney and wheeled out of the house.

Brooks turned to Maggie. "We're taking your car to the hospital. I'm driving."

Maggie rode along for the first few minutes in silence. When they left the city limits of Dogwood Mountain, the questions filled her mind. "Why is he being arrested?" she asked Brooks.

"Are you calm right now?" Brooks asked without looking in her direction.

"As calm as I can be," Maggie admitted.

"Okay," Brooks said. "A car was found abandoned out where the highway divides down by the river. There was a male occupant, dead. Single stab wound. Bled to death."

"Oh, gosh." Maggie pinched her eyes closed, fearful of what would come next.

"The victim was clutching your son's dog tags in his hand when he was discovered by the state highway patrol," Brooks said.

"What is the name of the victim?"

Brooks glanced over at her. "His name is Jeremy Justin McCoy, goes by J.J."

"Okay, and you arrested my son because his dog tags were in the guy's hand?"

Brooks nodded. "You have to know that it makes him the primary suspect."

Maggie gripped the door handle. She closed her eyes tighter and let out a long, moaning cry. "No," she wailed.

"Maggie, Maggie!" Brooks had pulled the car into the hospital parking lot. He stopped close to the entrance. "He was only just arrested. There has to be an investigation. You know how this goes."

"Right now, your daughter-in-law and grandchild are in the ambulance. We need to stay focused on that."

She bit the inside of her lip to keep herself calm. "I wonder what could be wrong with them, Cynthia and the baby," she said. Her voice was thick and shaky.

Brooks turned the car off and handed the keys back to her. "This is where we put on a brave face and we go in and find out," he said.

Maggie nodded and opened her car door. She followed Brooks through the emergency room doors and approached the reception desk.

"Can I help you?" the young woman behind the glass partition asked.

"I'm here to see about my daughter-in-law, Cynthia Sharpe," Maggie said stiffly. "She's pregnant and was just brought in by ambulance."

"I'm sorry, Miss, but unless you are a direct family member, you aren't allowed in to see her," the young woman said.

Immediately, Brooks pulled his wallet from his pocket then flashed his police badge to the young woman.

"Officer Brooks Macklin, Dogwood Mountain Police Department, ma'am," he said. "Please be advised that I brought this woman here in my company to visit the patient. If you have any concerns, please contact my Chief, Brett Mission, at this number." He pushed a business card across the desk to her.

"Wait here," she said and stood up from her desk. Maggie was unsure where she went, but when she returned she was smiling. "Okay, Officer Macklin. You may accompany your companion back to the nurses' station. They will direct you from there."

Maggie said nothing but inwardly seethed at the fact that it took a police officer to give her access to her new family. They walked through a set of double doors and met a smiling woman in blue scrubs when they entered the emergency department.

"Officer Macklin?" She stood in front of Brooks as he nodded. "If you'll follow me to the waiting room over here."

Maggie walked behind him and waited until they reached the small seating area. The nurse closed a curtain around them and gestured toward the empty chairs. "We need you to listen for a minute." She turned to Maggie. "Cynthia was taken into labor and delivery as soon as she was brought in, about ten minutes ago. She is in active labor and will be delivering her baby before long."

"Is everything okay? I mean, the baby has to be early, right?" Maggie hugged herself around her middle and rocked slightly. Less than a day ago she had no idea that she was going to be a grandmother. And now, she was on the verge of tears praying internally for the health and well-being of the little life she just found out was about to come into the world.

"Please continue to wait here and someone will come and get you when you can see her," the nurse said.

"Officer Macklin, you are welcome to wait as well, or you can leave Ms. Sharpe. She is welcome to stay unless the other Mrs. Sharpe has other plans."

Brooks extended his hand toward Maggie and led her toward a set of chairs. He made sure she was settled in and told her he'd be back soon.

CHAPTER SIX

After Brooks left, Maggie sat in the waiting room, trying to calm her fears a bit for Cynthia and the baby, but her heart beat in a hollow space when she allowed herself to think about Bradley. The nurse that brought her there peeked her head through the curtain into the seating area. "You can come on up to the labor and delivery floor if you would like to, Ms. Sharpe."

Maggie rose from her chair to follow the nurse. They walked past several rooms to the back of the emergency department to a set of elevators. Maggie said nothing when the nurse pushed the button for the third floor.

"To get in and out here, you need to enter a code," the nurse explained. She punched in a four-digit code and waited while the door clicked open. "I'll write it down for you."

"Thanks," Maggie said. She followed her through the hallway and around a corner to a large room. She knocked on a wide wooden door and waited for the nurse inside the room to respond.

"I have Maggie Sharpe here to see Cynthia Sharpe," the first nurse said. They waited while the second nurse turned back to the room.

"She can come in," the nurse said. Maggie noted the name "Angie" on her tag.

"Thanks," Maggie said to the first nurse, and then followed Angie into the room. When she entered, Cynthia was sitting upright on the hospital bed. Her clothing had been replaced by a typical hospital gown.

Maggie forced a smile on her face. "How are you?" she asked.

"Miserable," Cynthia said. "I'm in pain and I want medication."

"You have to be patient, Cynthia," Angie said. "You have to wait and let us figure out what we're going to do."

Maggie turned to the nurse. "Is there anything you can give her? She is in pain, right?"

Angie nodded. "She is in active labor, so yes, she is in pain. But we need to monitor the baby for a little while before we can determine what will be safe to give her."

"Active labor," Maggie said. "Isn't it too early for that?"

"I need something for the pain," Cynthia wailed.

"She is full-term," Angie said. "This baby is coming soon."

"Full-term," Maggie muttered to herself. She was stunned by the news but quickly dismissed it when Cynthia reared her head back and moaned in pain.

"Okay, we're going to need to get you examined again." Angie tightened a strap around Cynthia's abdomen and threw back the sheet over her legs. Maggie turned around in time to miss anything she didn't want to see.

"Is everything okay?" Cynthia cried. "Is my baby okay?"

"Your baby is about to be born," Angie said.

"Should I leave?" Maggie asked.

"You should run out to the nurses' station and tell Dr. Cooper that we need her in here as soon as possible," Angie said.

Maggie took off as fast as she could. She threw the door open and headed back around the corner. She reached the desk where several people in scrubs were standing around. "I need Dr. Cooper," she gasped. "The nurse in the other room, Angie, said to come out and get him into the room where my daughter-in-law is."

An older woman stood up and grabbed the receiver of the desk phone in front of her. "Who is the patient?"

"Cynthia Sharpe," Maggie said. "Should I go back?"

"No," the older nurse said. "Go to the waiting room and wait for someone to come and get you or call you."

Instead, Maggie headed toward the elevators and pushed the button for the ground level. She went back through the main part of the hospital and back toward the parking lot where Brooks had left her car. She looked around for any sign of him when she walked back out into the night. If there was anything she could do to let her son know that his child was about to be born, she was going to try to do it.

"Maggie," Brett called to her before she could see him in the parking lot. She looked around and spotted him standing next to her car. "How is she?"

"What do you care?" she snapped. The words popped out of her mouth before she thought. "Why are you even here?"

"Come on, Maggie," Brett said. He took a step toward her. "You know I have a job to do. I don't want you to be angry with me for doing what I had to do. I didn't come here to bother you. I came here to get Brooks and check in on things."

She dropped her head. "In the past six hours I have been surprised with a visit from the son I haven't seen in over a year, met his wife and learned that they were going to have a baby, and watched as my son got arrested," she said. "I hope you will understand that I am in a very unsocial state of mind."

"Maggie." He placed his hand on her arm. He stepped in closer and turned her body toward his. Before she could resist, he circled her in his arms and pulled her close to him. She waited for a long second before she pushed him back off.

"I have to go," she said, pushing back. "Cynthia is about to deliver the baby. She is in labor right now. And apparently, I have to get my son an attorney."

Brett cleared his throat. "I'm sorry. I know that you are hurting right now, even if I am the one who is causing the hurt," he said. "I informed your son's commanding officer about his arrest. He has not been formally charged just yet. I arrested him on suspicion. The Navy will be sending an attorney as soon as possible. Right now, you need to focus on that baby."

"I plan to focus on the baby," Maggie said defensively. "Even if I did just find out that he or she existed."

"Either way, being born early like this is not good," Brett said. "The baby could be in the hospital for a very long time."

Maggie didn't want to share what she knew about the baby being full term yet. There was already more than enough going on and she didn't much feel like sharing the details with anyone about anything right now. She wanted to keep her distance from Brett, too. Even if she knew he had a job to do, it hurt her to see her boyfriend arrest her son. The last thing she wanted to do was stir up more of a mess by getting angry with him or saying something she'd regret.

CHAPTER SEVEN

The next morning, Maggie planned to spend time at the donut shop getting ready for the day before leaving to head for the county jail, which is where Brooks had informed her Bradley had been moved.

"You go on and do what you need to do," Ruby told her. "We can handle it here."

"No," Maggie said. "I need to stay busy. I'm not needed at the hospital, and I can't go see Bradley until nine."

"Why aren't you needed at the hospital?" Myra asked her.

"Because my daughter-in-law wanted to be alone," she said. "I haven't even had the chance to see the baby yet."

"You haven't?" Ruby frowned and leaned against the sink. "Do you know the gender?"

Maggie shook her head. "I haven't heard a thing. I'm worried about that," she said. "I'm worried that something might be wrong."

"How early was the baby?" Ruby asked.

"I don't want to talk about it right now," Maggie said.

"Okay. I only mentioned it because Orson was asking Brett some questions and…"

"Brett has no right to say a word," Maggie said, trembling. She'd never been happier to have made the decision not to tell him that the baby was full term. Even now, while she felt guilty for not sharing the truth with her very best friend in the world, Maggie couldn't settle her mind long enough to focus on the topic.

"I know you're angry with him. You would have to be," Ruby said. "But look at it from his perspective."

"Why? Why do I have to look at it from his perspective?" Maggie railed. "He is a cop, and he arrested my son."

"He's just doing what he has to do," Ruby said. "Surely you understand that. You two are in a relationship and you'd do well to remember that."

Maggie groaned and hung her head. She knew she deserved the reality check and even though the words stung, Ruby was right. She was angry about a lot of things, and even finding that her feelings were hurt, and she was just looking for someone to blame.

"You're right and I know that, but it doesn't make this any easier. All I want to do right now is go see my son. I hope that's okay, and that you aren't too upset with me for not wanting to talk." She held out her hand to her friend, a look settling on her face that couldn't be mistaken as anything but pain and confusion. Ruby took her hand and brought her in for a hug.

She packed up her purse and headed out the door to her car. It was early, but she didn't care. Later, Maggie knew she would have an apology to make to her best friend. Ruby would understand. That's what friends are for.

She arrived at the jail with fifteen minutes to spare. With her head in her hand, she leaned against the steering wheel and tried her best to gather her thoughts. Less than two days ago, her world chugged along like a slow-moving train. Between her donut shop and her friends, she had what she needed.

Now, it had all been thrown into chaos. Not that she was unhappy to see her son, and although she was shocked at the news of his marriage and the new baby, she knew that eventually the shock would wear off and her life would be filled with more joy than she had ever known.

Maggie sat up tall and looked around her. The clock on her car stereo told her that she had twelve more minutes before she could even enter the jail for visitation. She had called ahead and informed the jail that she planned to visit her son. She decided to make use of the time she had left to call in and check on the baby. She searched for the hospital's main phone number and waited while the operator transferred her to the labor and delivery department.

"Labor and delivery," the nurse answered.

"Hi. I'm calling to check on Cynthia Sharpe," Maggie said. "I was with her yesterday while she was in labor. I am her mother-in-law. When I left the baby was on its way and I was just wondering how things were going."

"I'm sorry, but we are unable to give out patient information over the phone," the nurse said.

"Okay, I understand that, but can you at least confirm that the baby and mom are okay?"

"Again, ma'am, we require a code before you can receive any information," the nurse said.

"Oh," Maggie said. "You didn't mention a code. I have the code the nurse named Angie gave me yesterday to get in and out of the ward." She searched her bag for the slip of paper the nurse had given her and read the code over the phone.

"I'm sorry," the nurse said at last. "Even though you have the correct code, this patient has a 'no outside contact' request on file."

"Wait, I'm confused," Maggie said. She felt the knots in her stomach tighten. "You just said I needed the code, and now you're telling me that even with the code I can't find anything out about my grandchild or daughter-in-law?"

"That's what I am telling you, ma'am," the nurse said. "And to save yourself some time with your next question, this also applies to visitors. Your daughter-in-law has explicitly requested that. I'm sorry, but I can't give you any more information than that."

"Can you tell me the gender of the baby?"

"No, ma'am, I cannot," the nurse said. Her tone stiffened. "I cannot tell you anything about mother or baby."

"But the baby is here, and is okay?" Maggie pressed further. "You can confirm that?"

The nurse sighed. "I can only tell you that there is a baby," she said and sighed again. "And I can say that, in general, if we have any babies that are born sick they are transferred to the neonatal intensive care unit in Joplin. That's all I can say, alright? If you want any more information, you are going to have to get Mrs. Sharpe's permission for that."

The phone disconnected. Maggie shook her head and opened up her car door. If Bradley had questions

CHAPTER EIGHT

Maggie entered the public entrance to the county jail and checked in with the receptionist up front. She waited in the waiting area until a uniformed guard called her back through a set of doors. "First, go through here." She pointed toward a metal detector. "Then I'm going to need to search your person before you are allowed back further," the guard said. "Stand up and hold your arms out to the side," she ordered next. Maggie did as she was asked. The guard searched her and then directed her down the hall. When she reached the end, another guard stood holding open a door to a small room.

"Who are you here to see?" another female guard asked.

"Bradley Sharpe," Maggie replied.

"Do you have an appointment?" the guard asked without looking at her.

"I called yesterday afternoon," Maggie said. "My name is Maggie Sharpe."

"This way, please," the woman said and directed her to a chair in front of a small cubicle. "When the prisoner arrives, you will reach for the phone receiver and speak into it. Keep your hands off of the glass partition. Nudity and explicit talk are not allowed…"

"Good grief," Maggie gasped. "I'm his mom!"

This time, the guard's eyes rose to meet hers. "Lady, how long have you worked in corrections?"

"I've never worked in corrections," Maggie replied.

"Well, if you ever do, you'll understand why we say that line to everyone who comes in, and I do mean everyone," she said. "By the way, your conversation might be recorded. There is no expectation of privacy here."

"Thank you for the head's up," Maggie said. She took a seat and lifted her eyes to meet the guards' again.

"Can I ask, why was I searched if there is no contact between myself and the prisoner?"

"Are you close enough to me that you can hurt me?" the guard asked.

Maggie nodded. "Point taken."

The guard smiled and picked up the two-way radio attached to her uniform. She rattled off a code and a series of instructions. Maggie heard her son's name, but otherwise understood little of the exchange. The guard glanced at the clock high up on the wall. "It will be about ten minutes before he is brought in," she said. After a moment, she addressed Maggie again. "Tell me something now, what do you do for a living?"

"I run a donut shop in Dogwood Mountain," Maggie said.

"Do you own it?" the guard asked.

Maggie nodded. "It was my aunt's," she explained. "Why do you ask?"

"I was just curious. I figure you and I are about the same age. I sometimes wonder what other women my age do for a living," she said. "And you're not the normal type I see around here."

Maggie was unsure how to take the comment. "What type do you normally see?"

The guard laughed. "The type we have to explain all of those instructions to," she said.

Maggie wanted to ask more questions, but she hesitated when she heard the sound of footsteps. She glanced up when the door on the other side of the glass opened and another guard led her son into the room. He was dressed in a pair of gray scrubs similar to the nurses she had seen at the hospital.

He sat across the glass from her and picked up the phone receiver.

"Mom," he said, breathing heavily into the phone. "Have you heard anything from Cynthia?"

Maggie paused and looked into her son's eyes. "Son, she had the baby."

Bradley looked down and breathed deeply a few times before looking back up. "Oh no. Are they okay? How much did the baby weigh? Did they have to go to the NICU? Is it a boy or a girl? She wanted to be surprised."

She sighed and wished so badly that she could reach out to her son for a hug. "I don't know. I was at the hospital with her last night for a little while, but they asked me to leave and now they are telling me that she has requested no contact," she said. "The nurse told me that she will not accept visitors, either."

Bradley had been seated forward in his chair, eager to talk with his mom. As she spoke, he sat back in his chair. His shoulders slumped. "I don't understand," he said. "Why wouldn't she want visitors?"

Maggie forced herself to smile. She held back her thoughts about the matter. "I can only imagine what it must be like for her to have a baby in a place that isn't her home, all alone without you by her side," she said.

"Do you think that's all it is, Mom?" Bradley asked. "We got married so fast and please don't be mad at me for this, but we didn't know each other all that well to begin with. In fact, we're still learning a lot about each other now."

"You all lost touch after you got back aboard the ship?"

Bradley nodded. "I hadn't spoken to her for months, and then she asked to meet with me when I had any leave," he said. "She told me about the baby, so we got married almost the minute I got off the ship."

"Wait," Maggie said. "You had no other contact with her between the time you met in Japan and when you saw her and got married?"

"Don't judge me, Mom," he said. "I did what was right. I may not have known that she was pregnant, but the second I found out I wrote to her and asked for her hand in marriage."

"I'll do what I can to reach out to her." Maggie smiled as brightly as she could muster. "I will come back as soon as I can with photos and news about Cynthia and the baby." She said the words, but barely believed them herself.

"If it's a boy, we said we'd name him Wyatt and if it's a little girl, we'd name her Olivia. Please, find out what you can." He held his hand up against the glass.

Maggie met his hand and swore she could feel his feelings even through the cold separation of the glass. "Of course, and in the meantime, you have your meeting with your attorney from the Navy and then you can fill me in on what they have to say."

"The J.A.G. lawyer was here earlier and dropped off some paperwork, but I haven't gotten the chance to meet her yet."

"What is a 'jag'?" Maggie asked.

"It stands for 'judge advocate general' and it's the official name of the attorney," he said.

"Is there anything you can tell me about what's going on?" She looked around, unsure what she was even allowed to say.

"I don't know much at all yet. All I know is that I hate that all of this is happening. Please go find out everything you can about Cynthia and the baby and come back as soon as you can, Mama," Bradley whispered into the receiver. "This place is awful."

Maggie felt a pang in her chest when he called her "mama."

CHAPTER NINE

Maggie pulled back into the alley behind the donut shop a little after ten. Her arms and legs ached, and she wanted nothing more than to drive home and fall into her bed. But her responsibilities at the donut shop called to her, and she felt that she owed at least one person there an apology.

"How did it go?" Ruby asked her the minute she stepped through the back door.

"His naval attorney dropped off some paperwork earlier," Maggie said. "He was also concerned about Cynthia and the baby, of course."

"Had he heard anything?"

Maggie shook her head. "He's not able to receive

messages inside the jail," she explained. "He did tell me that they hadn't spoken a whole lot since their initial meeting in Japan."

Ruby rested against the cooler door and folded her arms. "Wait a minute, they are married," she said. "How did they get from not talking much to being married with a new baby?"

Maggie shook her head and closed her eyes. "I don't know how to explain it, Ruby," she said. "We didn't have much time to talk, and of course, I thought of twenty more questions to ask him after our visit was over." She sighed heavily. "It almost sounded like she wrote to him and informed him about the baby and then they got married as soon as he was free on leave."

"What did he say about the charges against him?"

The question stunned her for a moment. "We didn't even talk about it," she said. "I never asked, and he didn't bring it up. He was so much more concerned about the baby and his wife."

"Did you happen to see Brett while you were there?"

Maggie's face fell. "No, that was last night," she said. "He met me in the hospital parking lot, and he talked about how the baby is early and how he had no choice but to slap the cuffs on my son and throw him in jail."

"Wait, wait," Ruby said. "How did Brett know that the baby was early?"

Maggie inhaled a breath. It was time to tell Ruby the truth, or at least what she thought she knew. "I assumed he got the idea from Bradley, but the weird thing is, the nurse said at the hospital that the baby was full term."

Ruby's eyes were wide. "And what did Cynthia say?"

"She didn't say either way," Maggie said. "It was so fast. I was shooed away from her room very quickly. I just don't know."

"None of this makes sense." Ruby frowned. "How are you holding up?"

Maggie pushed herself off of the wall she had been leaning against and headed for the baker's table where her apron was folded up. "I need to get busy," she said. "I left you here holding down the fort."

"That's what I'm here for." Ruby returned to the prep table where she was putting the finishing touches on the day's lunch boxes.

"No," Maggie held up a hand. "I was short with you this morning. In my heart, I felt disconnected from you and this place, and that's not right. I don't know where I would be without you and your friendship. And especially now, when my life has been thrown upside down, I shouldn't be pushing you away."

"You know, part of that being there for each other like family means you don't have to make apologies," Ruby said. "You still do it because that's the kind of good egg you are. But you don't have to."

Maggie nodded her head and smiled. "Thanks, Ruby," she said and began mixing a new batch of sweet roll dough.

They worked in silence for several minutes. Orson stomped through the swinging door and threw his hands over his head. "They're coming out of the woodwork," he grumbled. "There's another one out there for you."

Maggie looked around the room for a moment. "Are you talking to me?"

"Of course, I'm talking to you," Orson said. "There's yet another young man out there asking for you, who claims to be in the Navy and interested in your son."

Maggie wiped her hands off on her apron and headed past the grumpy old man. She burst through the swinging door and stopped just short of the front counter. A young man, this time in uniform, stood on the other side of the counter. He held his uniform cap in his hand. Like Bradley, his dark hair was cut close to his head.

"I'm Maggie Sharpe."

"Hello, ma'am," the younger man said. "I'm Pete DeLuca, one of the guys that serves with your son. I heard that he is in some trouble."

"Come on outside with me." Maggie wasn't sure what the rest of the small town she lived in had heard about her son, and she was in no hurry to broadcast his unfortunate situation.

"Yes, ma'am." Pete followed her out into the parking lot.

When they were outside Maggie turned to him. "Are you friends with Bradley?" she asked. "What do you know about what's going on?"

"I know that he was arrested for murder," Pete said. He shifted his weight to his right foot. Maggie was reminded of a first-grader asking to use the restroom. "And I know that his new wife is having a baby."

"She's had the baby, as far as I know," Maggie said.

"What do you mean, as far as you know?"

Maggie sighed. She wasn't sure how much she should share. "The hospital isn't allowing visitors at the moment," she said. "And you know, medical information and all."

Pete nodded his head. "Yeah. Do you know if I can visit Bradley?"

"I'm not sure," she said. "I had to call ahead and make arrangements to visit him this morning."

"You saw him this morning?" Pete asked.

"I figured he'd want to see his mom."

"Yeah, sure," Pete said. He seemed to be thinking. "I suppose he would want to see his mom."

"So, where are you from, Pete?"

"Oh, I grew up in Tulsa," he said.

"When did you join the Navy?" she asked.

"After high school. Did you say which hospital Cynthia was in?"

"I didn't," Maggie said. "But I'm sure Bradley will tell you when you see him. Why don't you come on back inside the donut shop and I'll treat you to something to eat and a cup of coffee, okay? And while you're eating, I'll get the number to the county jail for you."

She didn't wait for him to say another word. There was something about the questions he was asking that didn't sit right with her.

CHAPTER TEN

Maggie sent Pete off with the information to set up a visit at the county jail. After she watched him leave with his donuts and coffee in tow, she headed straight for the kitchen. "What was that all about?" Ruby asked her.

"He said he was a shipmate of Bradley's and wanted to speak with him. He also asked a lot of questions about Cynthia and the baby."

"What did you say?"

"I did my best to avoid giving too many details," Maggie said. "I feel like that's not my place, anyway."

"It's not like you've heard much of anything yourself as it is," Ruby said.

Maggie shook her head and sighed. "I'm going to get back to work on these cinnamon rolls," she said and straightened her apron. She resumed the sweet roll dough. When it was time to knead the dough, she attacked it with vigor. With each fold, she pressed her frustrations into the dough for ten minutes. When she was finished, she looked up to meet Ruby's grin.

"Feel better?"

"Not yet," Maggie said. "Where is Orson? He said something earlier that's been bothering me."

"What did he say?"

"When that guy showed up for Bradley, Orson said 'they're coming out of the woodwork.' Does that mean there have been others showing up here asking for Bradley?"

"Was there another guy here for your son?" Myra asked, popping her head out of the office.

Maggie's quirked a brow and crossed her arms. "Are you talking about the guy who just left?"

Myra shrugged. "I'm talking about the guy who was here yesterday."

Maggie's head snapped up. She looked at Ruby and nearly shouted, "Who was he? What did he want?"

"Maggie," Ruby said and moved beside her. "Calm down a little bit. Why are you so worked up over this?"

Maggie hung her head. "I don't know," she said. "I just feel like my world is spinning out of control. Every time I find out another person might be involved it feels like a torpedo screaming toward my family out of left field."

"This guy didn't seem to be anything more than just a good buddy," Myra said. "He was just asking about Bradley and Cynthia."

"Exactly like the guy who just left here," Maggie said.

Ruby glanced over at the baker's table. "How long before that dough is ready to be rolled out?"

"Another forty-five minutes," Maggie said. "Why?"

"Because you and I are going to take a break. But we're going to do it in private." She marched into the office and pulled the keys to the food truck off of a hook on the wall. "Myra? Can you handle everything here?"

"Without a doubt," Myra promised.

"Alright." Ruby hooked her arm inside Maggie's and led her swiftly through the swinging door and the dining room. When they reached the parking lot she opened the food truck and gently pushed Maggie inside. "Sit," she commanded Maggie to take a seat at the small table, then began turning on the coffee maker.

"What are we doing out here?" Maggie asked. "I've been running all over the place over the past few days and leaving you here to run things. I know you could use some help to get caught up."

"What I could use is a chance to sit and talk to my best friend." Ruby poured two half cups of coffee from the small amount that had already been brewed. "I think we need to talk about what's been going on. Your son shows up and this whirlwind of news swirls past you, and here you are trying to understand everything that's happened."

"You can say that again. One minute I'm excited to see my son and the next minute I'm finding out that not only is he married but expecting a child. Or rather, has a child."

"Not to mention your son's arrest and the fact that you can't seem to get in touch with your daughter-in-law since she was taken to the hospital."

"Right, and all of these other people that seem to be coming out of nowhere."

"So, that's what we need to do here," Ruby said. "We need to talk through all of the things you know right now. A lot of this isn't adding up and you know things always make more sense when we talk them through."

Maggie nodded her head. "I also need to try and get in touch with my daughter-in-law," she said.

"Okay, start there." Ruby stood up and pulled open one of the cabinet doors. She took out a pad of paper and a pen.

She decided to text her over making a phone call. She doubted the new mother would answer her phone for an unfamiliar number.

"Cynthia, this is Maggie," she typed. "I'm so worried about you and the baby. I haven't heard anything new. Are you alright? Do you need anything?"

She waited for a reply. Her messaging app indicated that the message had been delivered and then read.

"Nothing?"

Maggie shook her head. "I don't understand any of this. It seems like there is more we don't know than we do know."

Ruby wrote a few words across the top of the page. "What we do know is that Bradley showed up here and some guy wound up dead in his rental car out on the highway with Bradley's dog tags in his hands."

"Right, and beyond that, what else is there?"

"Well." Ruby cocked her head to the side. "We know that Cynthia is acting weird since she went to the hospital."

"Do you think she has anything to do with that young man's death? Did she know J.J. somehow?"

"We have no way to know that right now, but we do know that she has acted strangely since the birth of the baby. And we also know that there might be something off about the baby's due date and how long she's been pregnant."

Maggie's eyes widened when her phone buzzed. "She messaged me back."

"What does it say?" Ruby asked, practically jumping out of her chair.

"Please allow me some space for the time being. We are out of the hospital and back at the bed and breakfast, but I will not be accepting visitors until further notice," Maggie read.

"Whoa, that just sounds contrived," Ruby said. "Something isn't right here."

"No, but if they're already out of the hospital, the baby must be okay." She let out a huge sigh of relief. As annoyed as she was about how Cynthia was acting, she was thankful. "I'm going ask her about the baby." Maggie began typing once again. "I think I deserve to know if the baby is alright at the very least."

"And maybe whether you're the grandmother of a boy or a girl," Ruby mumbled.

The phone pinged again, and Maggie read the reply. "Baby is fine. We are both fine. We just need some time."

"Ask her about the gender," Ruby urged.

Maggie typed once more. "I'm sure they need some things," she said as she typed. "I'm offering to go and get her some supplies and drop them off. Albert can see to it that they get to her. I don't have to see them just yet."

"You're being way nicer about this than I would be," Ruby admitted. She sipped her coffee but the scowl on her face was hard to hide.

"I'm being nicer than I want to be, but sometimes kindness is what gets you farther in life and right now, I can't afford to argue with this woman." Maggie, more determined than ever, knew that she had to keep her wits about her before something else went truly wrong.

CHAPTER ELEVEN

After lunch, Maggie drove downtown to the small dime store in the middle of town. Down the baby aisle she walked, selecting any newborn-sized outfit she could that could work for a little boy or a little girl. It would have been much easier if Cynthia was more forthcoming with information, but of course, she was not.

She avoided pink and blue and then moved on to receiving blankets, pacifiers, diapers, wipes, and even a few bottles.

When she finished shopping, she drove back by the donut shop at Ruby's request and picked her up. Together they drove across town and up the hill to the large estate house that overlooked the rest of the small

Ozark town. Maggie had finally gotten used to calling the old house the Dogwood House. Like her own small cottage in town and the donut shop itself, the property had once belonged to her late Aunt Marjorie Getz.

The house was now owned by Gretchen LeClair, who had turned it into a successful bed and breakfast. Maggie thought about how Aunt Marjorie's flesh and blood was sleeping somewhere in that same house right now. Of course, Maggie could only hope she would be allowed to see the small baby that had just extended her family.

"Do you think she'll accept what you're bringing her?" Ruby asked when they drove up the hill.

Maggie moved her head slowly from side to side. "Honestly, Ruby, I have no idea," she said. "I don't know a thing about this woman my son just married. I also don't know a thing about my grandchild. But I had to do what I thought was right to do. This felt like the right thing."

"With Bradley behind bars, it seems to me like it's the only thing you can do," Ruby agreed.

"I also want to chat with Gretchen in person," Maggie said. "I have no idea how long the kids planned to stay here. Their room might not be paid for at the moment and Cynthia may not have the funds to cover it."

"So, you were thinking that you would work it out with Gretchen to pay for their stay until the matter with Bradley can be resolved?"

"If the matter with my son can be resolved." Maggie turned into the driveway and glanced over at her friend. Maggie was caught up in her thoughts about the murder charge that was sure to be filed against her only child.

"I don't want you to be mad at me," Ruby said. She folded her hands under her chin and smiled. "But I talked with Gretchen myself this morning and paid ahead for their room."

Her first reaction was to be surprised, but Maggie was quickly wiping the tears from her eyes. "You did what? Why would you pay for the kids' room?"

"Because I got to thinking about the same thing, wondering how long their money would last them with Bradley in jail," she said. "And I am in a much better position to do that. The donut shop is booming. I know that as well as you. But owning a small business doesn't make you wealthy. After buying the food truck, I had a feeling that you might be a little cash strapped."

"I will pay you back," Maggie said weakly.

"No, you will not," Ruby ordered. "What you are going to do is understand that you are family to me now, and so is that kid of yours, and now his kid, I suppose!" She laughed and slid her arm around her best friend's shoulders.

"Thank you," Maggie said firmly. She inhaled deeply and wiped the tears from her eyes. "Let's go deliver this stuff to the little boy or little girl waiting on the other side of that door."

Maggie parked in the driveway and popped the latch to the trunk of her car. She grabbed an armful of bags. Ruby did the same.

"What are you two ladies doing here on such a warm afternoon?" Albert Boudreaux, Gretchen's groundskeeper and all-around helper, greeted them.

"We are here to deliver these things to the new baby," Maggie said. "Is Gretchen around?"

"No, ma'am." Albert shook his head. His mellow southern Louisiana accent softened his words. "Miss Gretchen ran off to her eye doctor this afternoon. She said it would be good to let mama and baby have a little time this afternoon to sleep. That rascal kept his mama up all night last night."

Maggie felt her heart catch in her throat. "His?"

Albert pursed his lips. "Now, I understand how the young lady wants to keep it all hidden from everyone just now," he said. "And I know that the young man she came here with is in jail over something he couldn't have done. And I know that young man is your boy, Miss Sharpe. But that baby is a boy, as I am an old firecracker from the bayou. He's a little boy who's not really little." Albert broke into a fit of laughter.

"Have you seen the baby yourself, then?" Ruby asked.

Albert nodded his head deeply. "Yes, ma'am. Seen and held the poor little fella while his mama took a long shower. He is a strong, big boy. I'd say he weighs every bit of ten pounds, that one."

"You said that you know my son couldn't have done what he is in jail for, Albert," Maggie said. "How do you know that? Can you tell me why you said that?"

"I know because that night the other young man was killed out on the highway, your boy stayed right here sound asleep," Albert said. "I was up that night having one of my fits of insomnia. I walk the grounds around here when the weather allows for it on those nights. Sometimes the night air comes along and helps me get back to sleep."

"And you didn't see the car leave the driveway?" Maggie asked hopefully. "Is that what you're saying?"

Albert shook his head. "No, ma'am. I am not saying that at all," he corrected. "I did see their rental car leave this driveway early in the wee hours of the morning. But it wasn't Mr. Sharpe who was driving. I know that for sure."

"How do you know? Did you see the driver?"

"Not up close, but whoever it was couldn't have been your boy, ma'am," Albert said. "Your boy is a good head taller than the person who drove off in their car in the middle of the night."

"Albert," Maggie said. She was suddenly out of breath. "Have you had the chance to talk to the police about this fact? Have you reached out to anyone and let them know this?"

Albert nodded his head. "Yes, I did, but I didn't have to reach out to them. Chief Mission came around here almost as soon as that boy of yours landed in the county jail and started asking me all kinds of questions. He wrote down everything I had to say and then took off."

"I wonder if you provided the key to unlock my son's jail cell," Maggie said. Although, she wondered too why he was still there with Albert's information.

"Well, Chief warned me not to expect a miracle too soon," Albert said. "I told young Mrs. Sharpe the same thing this very morning. The Chief told me that it was out of his hands now how soon the charges were filed or dropped against your son. He said that it was up to the sheriff now since the murder took place out on the highway and not within the city limits."

"Then why was Brett the one who arrested him?" Ruby asked.

"Well, that I can tell you." Albert smiled. "Chief Mission told me himself that he asked the sheriff to let him come and get the boy himself, knowing that they were here in town. He said that he didn't want some well-meaning deputy to rough over that boy. You know people can be like that, thinking that they're acting out of some loyalty to the dead. But your boy is a member of the Navy, and he deserves to be treated right."

Maggie was too stunned to speak. Ruby thanked Albert for her and followed him up on the porch where they decided to leave the baby things for Cynthia.

"I will let Miss Gretchen see to it that these things get to the young lady." Albert sighed and then leaned on the shovel still in his hands. "It's not proper, you know. I am way out of my lane to say such things, but it isn't proper for you to be kept from that little one, ma'am."

Maggie nodded her agreement. She reached out and patted the older man on the arm. "Thank you, Albert," she said.

CHAPTER TWELVE

"It's a boy," Maggie said as they drove back to the donut shop. "I can't believe that it's a boy."

"I'm so glad we finally know, but I think there's something we have to consider."

"What's that?" Maggie asked. Her mind was still reeling from the visit with Albert.

"If your son is under the impression that this baby is early..." Ruby shifted in her seat to look directly at her friend. "If the child isn't premature..." She was having a hard time getting the words out. "Albert himself is the second one to confirm that he most certainly was not born early."

"I'm hearing you, Ruby," Maggie said. "And I know

what you're trying to say. It's possible that the baby isn't Bradley's. But do you understand what that means for him?"

Ruby nodded. "I can only begin to imagine how devastating it will be to him to figure out that the woman he married did not deliver his child."

"Not just that," Maggie said. "If this McCoy kid had anything to do with Cynthia before all of this, it could make Bradley look guilty. If Bradley knew about the baby, or if he somehow found out. Who knows? But it can't be good."

"What I want to know is why this J.J. McCoy was even anywhere near Dogwood Mountain in the first place. This other guy, Pete? Maybe he legitimately came here out of concern over Bradley's situation. But southern Missouri is an awful random place to be unless you have a reason to be here."

Maggie nodded. "I've been thinking about that, too," she said. "I have been thinking about a lot of things."

Ruby climbed out of the car and headed for the back door to the donut shop. "I'm going to make sure that everyone is set for the rest of the day. Myra already volunteered to close up for us," she said. "You go on home, and I will be along as soon as I can."

"What are your plans?" Maggie asked.

"For starters, we're going dig deep into any one of these people's lives we can and see what we find," Ruby said. "And after that, I'm going to nail Orson down for a description of this mysterious other person he's seen hanging around. Maybe then we can come up with answers."

Maggie nodded. "Sounds like a plan," she said. "It's nice to feel like we have a plan."

She left Ruby at the donut shop and drove the short distance to her house. Maggie headed straight for the bathroom and peeled off her clothes. She stepped in the shower and let the water wash off her anxiety.

She stepped out and pulled on a new shirt and yoga pants when she heard Ruby make her way inside. "I'll be out in a second," Maggie shouted, surprised Ruby had arrived so quickly. She waited for Ruby's normal reply but never heard it.

Back out of the bathroom, Maggie twisted her hair into a bun at the base of her head. She threw her dirty clothes into the hamper in her room and headed for the kitchen. "Are you settled in, Ruby?"

Again, there was no reply. "Ruby?"

Maggie looked around the corner into the mudroom at the back of the house. Someone stood just inside the back door, but it was not Ruby. The figure was tall and dressed in jeans and a dark blue hooded sweat-shirt. From the body shape, she guessed the figure was a male. Maggie inhaled sharply and walked back-ward toward her dining room.

Her phone was still in her bedroom. She raced swiftly down the hall. When she returned to the kitchen the figure stood facing her. The light was at his back. "What are you doing here?" she demanded.

The hood concealed his face enough that Maggie couldn't see who it was.

"I've already called the police," Maggie warned.

She heard the back door open again. "There's some-body in here, Ruby," she called out.

"What in the-," Ruby shouted. Maggie forgot her fear and ran to the back of the house. When she reached the back door, Ruby was on the floor and the door was wide open.

"Are you hurt?" Maggie asked. She squatted down beside Ruby. "Did he do anything to you?"

"Nothing more than knocking me on my butt." Ruby rolled to her side and pushed herself up to her knees. "I'm fine, but you need to call Brett right away."

"Yeah," Maggie said, though she was less than enthusiastic about talking to the police chief. She dialed his number and expected to get his voicemail. But he answered right away.

"Maggie," he said, without a hello. "What's going on?"

"There was someone in my house," she said between gasps for air. She wasn't sure why the air seemed to have been pressed out of her lungs, but she found it difficult to breathe.

"Is he still there?" Brett asked.

"No, at least I don't think so," Maggie said. "Ruby showed up and frightened him off, I think."

"So, did Ruby see him?"

"I think she did," Maggie said. "I saw him, too. But he had on a hoodie, pulled down over his face."

"Maggie, give the phone to Ruby," Brett ordered. Maggie complied immediately. She handed her cell phone over to her friend and picked up a water bottle off the kitchen counter. She twisted off the lid and downed several swallows, forcing herself to calm down with each swig.

While Maggie drank her water, she heard Ruby describe the person that was in her house to Brett. "Yes, definitely male. No, his face was partially covered but I could tell that he was young, early twenties I would guess. The hood moved back once and I could see his hair color, but I didn't get a good enough look at his face that I think I could pick him out of a line-up if that answers your question."

Maggie stood just outside of the kitchen and leaned against the wall. She handed a new water bottle over to Ruby who unscrewed the cap and downed a few swallows while Brett spoke on the other end of the phone. "No," Ruby spoke again. "His hair was dark, black maybe. It was shaved close to his head."

The thought hit her at once. The dark hair and the shape of the parts of the face she did see formed a picture in her mind. "It was that kid that came to the donut shop looking for Bradley," she said. "Pete. Pete DeLuca was his name. He said he served on the same ship as Bradley, and he was asking me questions about the baby."

Ruby handed the phone back to Maggie. "Tell me what else you know about this kid," Brett said.

"He already knew about Bradley's arrest," Maggie said. "He said he grew up in Tulsa and joined the navy right out of high school. Aside from that, he had a lot of questions about Cynthia and the baby."

"Maggie, do you have any idea where he is staying? Did he mention anything about that?" Brett asked.

Maggie shook her head, and then remembered to answer him over the phone. "I have no clue, but Albert mentioned nothing about him when we dropped some things off for the baby at Dogwood House earlier."

"Did you speak with Cynthia, or see the baby?"

"No, Brett," Maggie said. "Cynthia still doesn't want to see anyone."

"Okay, here's what we need to do," Brett said. Maggie heard a car door open and the interior alarm beep indicating the keys were in the ignition. "I'm going to head that way and have a look around. You guys sit tight and wait for me. I'll take a more formal statement about the incident and the description."

"And after that?"

"After that, I'm going to pay the new mother a visit, whether she wants it or not," Brett said.

"Okay," Maggie said, then set the phone down on the table and slumped into the seat in front of it.

"Is Brett coming by?" Ruby asked.

Maggie nodded. "He'll be here in a few minutes."

Ruby pulled out a chair across from her and sat down. "How about you?" Ruby asked. "You look like you're about to pass out."

"It's just been a lot," Maggie said. "A lot to take in over the past little while."

"Sure, it has," Ruby agreed. "You just found out about the baby's gender, and then someone breaks into your house and leaves you feeling vulnerable."

"Not only that, but I think it's pretty clear that there is a problem with the timing of the baby's birth," Maggie said, finally admitting it. She looked up at her friend. "Is he even my son's child? And how evil am I for asking that question?"

"And I hate to say this." Ruby cringed. "But what if that Pete guy isn't a shipmate, after all?"

"You mean that he's someone from Cynthia's life?" Maggie asked. "Maybe they are all connected to Cynthia somehow and Bradley is just caught up with a bad crowd of people?"

"Maybe. I don't know what I mean, but obviously, something isn't right."

Maggie dropped her head into her hands. At this point, anything was possible and nearly every option was a bad one.

CHAPTER THIRTEEN

True to his word, Brett arrived at the house within minutes. He walked through the back door and searched around, and then took a look outside the back door.

"Is there anything else you can tell me about his description?" Brett asked them once again before he left.

"Nothing I can remember," Ruby said.

"Just the dark blue sweatshirt and jeans," Maggie said.

Brett waved before he got back in his personal vehicle. Maggie smiled slightly when she heard the engine in the old muscle car roar to life, thinking back to the simplicity of high school, long before life got too complicated. She was feeling bad after finding out Brett had chosen to arrest her son out of kindness, and she wanted to address it, but she needed to do it when they were alone. She owed him an apology and once everything finally settled down, she'd do just that. Right now, she needed answers and Brett had a job to do.

"How are you doing?" Ruby asked her.

Maggie nodded her head. "Still reeling, but I'm a little better," she said. "I wish I knew what Brett was thinking."

"Do you know what I'm thinking?" Ruby asked her.

"What, that we need to stick to making donuts instead of getting ourselves involved in these situations?" Maggie joked.

"Making jokes is a good sign. And let's not forget that many of these situations come to us, and not the other way around."

"Fair enough," Maggie said. "So, what were you thinking?"

"That we need to open up our computers and start looking pretty hard into these guys that have popped up since your son made his way back into town," Ruby said.

"I'm afraid we need to add Cynthia to that list as well."

"That's not all," Ruby said. "You remembered earlier what Orson had said when Pete showed up to ask questions, right? He spoke as if there had been more than one person to stop by the donut shop asking about Bradley. It's time we to talk to Orson and get a description."

"I'll throw something in the oven to sustain us," Maggie said. "And then I'll ask Orson to come by."

Maggie headed to the kitchen and turned the oven on. She pulled a few frozen appetizers out of her freezer and began arranging them on cookie sheets. Her mind went to the bottle of wine she had in the back of the fridge but decided quickly that coffee was a better choice.

"I texted Orson already," Ruby announced. She had gone back out to her truck and retrieved her laptop. She was already setting her computer up on the table when Maggie set a cup of coffee down in front of her. "Mmmm, coffee. That's exactly what I need right at the moment."

Maggie settled back into her seat with her laptop in front of her. "I should ask you how you're doing. You confronted the intruder yourself, while I have been sitting over here freaking out and didn't even ask you how you were," she said.

Ruby picked up her coffee and blew on it before she sipped. "I'm shaken, but fine," she said. "But I'm used to staring down ornery farm animals when they decide that they are in charge. Not much rattles me."

The chime on Maggie's phone alerted her to a new text message.

"Looks like Albert sent a message," she said and tapped the screen. A picture filled her screen. Maggie cried out and then covered her mouth with her hand.

"What is it?" Ruby demanded. She rose from her chair and walked around behind Maggie.

"Look, Ruby," Maggie said quietly. She pulled her hand away from her mouth and smiled at the cherubic face on the phone. "Albert must have snuck a picture when Brett was talking to Cynthia!"

"He's adorable," Ruby said, and then added with a chuckle, "And quite fat."

Maggie nodded and laughed. "I would say that he is definitely a large baby," she said. "So was Bradley."

Ruby returned to her seat. "There really is no delicate way to put this, but does he look like Bradley?" she asked.

Maggie turned the phone slightly. "I think so," she said. "I think I can see similarities, but I don't trust my own eyes right now." She gazed at the photo on her phone screen for several more moments before she turned her attention back to her laptop.

Ruby took the phone screen from her and studied the photo. "I could convince myself I see a family similarity in the eyes and mouth, but I can't be sure."

Maggie took the phone back and gazed at the tiny face on the screen for a minute longer. "I have to call Albert and thank him," she said.

"Maybe you ought to wait for a while. You don't want him to get caught. I'm sure his intentions were good, but still. He might have sent that photo to you without the mother's knowledge."

"Alright, then," Maggie said. She felt a calm resolve return to her mind. "I want to start looking into this young man my son supposedly murdered, and the other one who might have just broken into my house."

"I think I will take a look at your new daughter-in-law and see what I can find out," Ruby announced.

They sat in silence for several moments. Maggie started with a search of state court records. She looked for anything she could find on both J.J. McCoy and Pete Deluca.

Her search returned nothing worthwhile. Maggie stood up from the table and walked around the room. She stopped at the window and stared outside. "I need to clear my head a little bit," she said.

"For some reason, I thought that I would find court records on those two in the State of Missouri."

"But they're not from Missouri," Ruby said. "Understandable mistake. Didn't Deluca claim to be from Tulsa? Can you search records in Oklahoma?"

"I can do that," Maggie said and returned to her seat. She searched for the website and typed "Peter Deluca" in the space provided. "I can't find anything on him."

"I think there's only about a ten percent chance he told you the truth about being from Tulsa anyway," Ruby said. She stared hard at her screen. "Oh, no."

"What? Did you find something?" Maggie jumped up out of her chair again and stood behind her friend.

"I don't know what this means, but this isn't good. I found a photo that tagged Pete Deluca in it," Ruby said. "Is this the young man who spoke to you at the donut shop?"

Maggie leaned in and studied the image on the laptop screen. Cynthia stood on the bow of a small boat on some lake, smiling in the sunshine. Her red hair hung loosely over her fair shoulders. To her right stood a familiar face, a young man with black hair. His arm was draped over her shoulders.

"What on earth is Pete Deluca doing on a boat with my daughter-in-law?"

CHAPTER FOURTEEN

After Ruby took a screenshot of the image she found of Cynthia on the boat with Pete, she sent the image to Brett. Maggie texted Orson and asked him where he was. Her thoughts were clouded, but it felt like it'd been forever since they'd reached out to him. Within a few minutes, Orson came by with Myra and Brooks in tow. Brett pulled up in his car as they were coming inside.

"Looks like the gang's all here," Orson observed.

"I hope that you're okay with Brooks and I tagging along," Myra said. "We just wanted to check in with you and see how Cynthia and the baby were doing."

"Has anyone heard anything new about your son?" Brooks asked.

"You mean, you don't know? I thought you or Brett would know what is going on with him," Orson said.

Brett shook his head. "The county has him," he said. "We just picked him up. I'm not even sure where they are in their investigation."

"This is all such a mess," Maggie said. She threw her arms over her head. "My son shows up, married with a baby on the way, and then a moment later he gets arrested for murder."

Brett moved inside the house and hugged the back wall in the dining room. "Maggie, I am sorry about that," he said quietly. "I had to follow up, no matter who it is."

"I don't think anyone here doubts you for doing your job," Ruby said.

Maggie simply nodded her head and gave a weak smile. She returned to her seat at the table and waited while the others filed in and took seats themselves.

"Orson, you said something to Maggie about people coming out of the woodwork when Pete Deluca came into the donut shop," Ruby said. She pulled the photo up on her phone. "This is Pete. Have you seen another young person come in and ask about Bradley?"

Orson took the phone from her and tapped the photo. "This is the last one who came in," he said. "There was another one the other day. He was wearing a baseball cap pulled down over his face."

"Can you tell me what he said?" Brett cut in.

Orson shook his head. "About the same thing as this Pete guy said. He wanted to talk to Maggie about her son. He asked me a lot of questions, too. I suppose he wanted to find out what I knew."

"But Maggie wasn't there?" Brett asked.

Orson shook his head. "Nope, she was gone. I think I forgot to mention that this one stopped by," he said.

Brooks shot a look toward his boss. "Hey, Orson. Is it possible that the first guy was Pete? I mean, are you completely sure that they weren't the same person?"

Orson sat back and folded his arms. "Is this the part where you give me the not-so-subtle dementia test? Look, I met the first guy in the middle of a busy rush. I asked the second guy if he had been in before asking and he told me that he hadn't," he said. "I took his word for it."

"But is it possible that it was the same guy?" Brooks leaned forward and stretched his hand across the table. He gripped Orson lightly by the arm.

Orson unfolded his arms suddenly and slapped his palms on the tabletop. He opened his mouth to speak but closed it quickly. He stared off into space for a second and then focused on Brooks. "It could have been the same guy," he said, and then turned to Ruby. "Give me that phone again."

Ruby brought the photo back up on the screen and shoved it in front of him. Orson picked it up and held two fingers over the top of the guy's head, exposing just his nose and lower jaw.

"I really don't think it was the same guy." He handed the phone back to Ruby.

"Hold on a second," Maggie said. She turned her laptop screen to the rest of them. "I found another picture with both Cynthia and Pete Deluca," she said. "There are two other people with them. This one," she pointed to a man, "is tagged as J.J. McCoy and the other is tagged as Cal Boone, Cynthia's brother. It looks to me like Pete and Cynthia are awfully friendly, like they were dating or something."

"That's him!" Orson said. "The other guy is the one you identified as the brother. He was the one in the shop."

Ruby nodded slowly. "I think he's the one that was in the house, too. I'm almost a hundred percent sure of it."

Maggie remained as stoic as possible as her thoughts whirled. Were all these guys in on it? Whatever it was?

Brett walked out the back door for a moment and placed a phone call. When he returned, he looked at Brooks. "I just phoned in a description for both Deluca and Boone down at the station, but I was thinking about driving around to a couple of motels outside of town."

"Just to see if we can find anyone meeting their description," Brooks agreed. He stood up and placed his hand on Myra's shoulder. "We'll be back soon."

They stepped out the back door and headed for Brett's car. Before he could start the engine, Maggie heard the familiar ring of his cell phone. It was then that the engine roared to life, and the pair quickly left her driveway.

"I wonder if they got a hit on the whereabouts," Myra said.

Orson gripped the table with both hands and threw back his head. His laugh echoed off of the walls in the small house. "My dear, you have been hanging around that young man too much," he said. "You sound like a police officer yourself, or someone who plays one on television."

Myra burst out laughing, followed quickly by Ruby. Maggie tried to hold her laughter in, but gave up and joined in. She chuckled until tears poured down her face.

It felt good, like a release of emotion. She was grateful that it occurred with laughter and not a torrent of tears.

"I suppose we can confirm that you two are in fact dating?" Ruby asked.

Myra blushed and nodded her head. "We are. We just made it official," she said. Maggie's phone rang before she could add more.

"It's Brett," Maggie announced. She stepped into the kitchen to answer the phone.

"I need you to come down to the police station as fast as you can," Brett said.

"Okay, what's going on?" she asked.

"I don't have time to explain," he insisted. "Just get down here fast. Bring Ruby with you."

CHAPTER FIFTEEN

Maggie drove her car as fast as she safely could. She barely noticed Ruby in the passenger seat beside her. In her mind, Brett had told her that something awful had happened to her son in the county jail.

"Slow down, Maggie," Ruby said when she ran from her car. She recalled parking it in the police station parking lot, shutting off the headlights, and pulling the keys from the ignition. Beyond that, she had little awareness between the time she slammed her car door shut and sprinted through the police station doors.

"Brett!" she called out.

Brooks met her in the front lobby. "Over here," he called to them. "Chief Mission wants me to take the two of you back to his office."

"I shouldn't have called him Brett," Maggie muttered to Ruby as they walked behind Brooks through the hallway that led back to the chief's office.

"I don't think it matters," Ruby told her.

"In here," Brooks said. "Just wait a second." He walked back out of the office door and down the hall.

"I wonder what's going on," Ruby said when they were alone in the office.

"Don't ask me to speculate," Maggie said. "My mind is only conjuring bad scenarios."

"Maggie," Ruby said. She rested her hand on Maggie's arm. "I'm sure if there was something wrong at the county jail, they would call you directly, not wait for the police chief in a neighboring town to inform you."

"I hope that you're right," Maggie said.

The door opened then, and Brett appeared inside. Maggie noted that his gun was strapped to his hip and his badge was on his belt loop.

"What's happened?" Maggie asked. "Is my son alright?"

Brett rested his hip on the front of his desk. "As far as I know he is fine," he said. "But I have other news."

"What's going on?" Ruby interjected. "I think we need to hear this news before this poor woman goes out of her mind with worry."

Brett nodded and cleared his throat. "Before I left your house with Officer Brooks, I received a call that an arrest had been made at Dogwood House."

"Dogwood House," Maggie squeaked.

"Gretchen called the police to report a loud argument between one of her guests and a young man answering to Pete Deluca's description," Brett continued.

"He was there?" Ruby asked.

"Apparently, he was staying in the room with Cynthia," Brett said quietly.

"Cynthia," Maggie repeated. "He was with Cynthia? And the baby?"

"That's the way it appears," Brett said. "At the very least, we have him on a charge of trespassing. He was not permitted to be staying there. Gretchen is pretty adamant about keeping a list of all the guests staying at the bed and breakfast.

"Where are Cynthia and the baby now?" Maggie asked. She felt her heart rate quicken as he spoke.

"That's why I called you down here, Maggie," Brett said softly. "Cynthia was arrested along with Deluca. According to the arresting officer, both of them fought back when Albert tried to figure out what was going on."

"Where is the baby, Brett?" Maggie asked.

"That's why you're here." The door opened once again. Brooks entered the room with the large diaper bag Maggie had purchased for Cynthia on his shoulder and the infant car seat in his arms.

"You're going to need to run to the grocery store for infant formula," Brett was saying.

Maggie heard, but her attention was on the tiny figure wiggling under a light blanket.

"Was she breastfeeding?" Ruby asked over her head.

"I think she had tried, but the baby wasn't really taking to it," Brett answered. They spoke in the background. Maggie's full attention was on her grandson.

"Did she give him a name?" she asked, remembering that Bradley had said if it was a boy, they'd name him Wyatt. She looked up from where she was kneeling on the floor beside the car seat. "What is his name?"

Brett rose from his desk and squatted on the floor beside her. He reached out and stroked the little boy's head. "I don't know that she'd even picked one yet," he said. "I called you down here, so he doesn't end up in the system tonight."

Maggie looked up and smiled at him through her tears. "Thanks for calling me."

Brett nodded. The baby gripped his finger in his tiny hand.

"What about Cynthia?" Maggie had to know.

Brooks spoke up. "She might not be released for some time, Maggie," he said.

Brett nodded. "Cynthia has a few questions to answer," he said. "We have some new information about the night J.J. McCoy was murdered."

"Information like what?"

Brett gently released his finger from the baby's grip. "For one, Albert saw their rental car leave late that night, within a couple of hours of the estimated time of death. But he said that Bradley wasn't the one driving."

"Who did he see driving?"

"Another man along with a very pregnant redhead," Brett said.

"You mean Cynthia and Pete?" Maggie blurted. "Oh, my gosh."

"We don't know what happened yet, but I wouldn't be surprised if your son isn't released soon," Brett told her.

Maggie gazed at the small face sleeping peacefully in the car seat. "I think we need to get this little boy home for the night," she said.

"What are you going to call him?" Brett asked.

"Wyatt." Maggie smiled. "Bradley said that's what they wanted to name him, so I'll go with that for now."

"That's a strong name for a beautiful little boy." Brett leaned in and gave Maggie a hug as a tear slid down her cheek. "You three get out of here and I'll give you a call soon."

"I'm glad you're with me," Maggie told Ruby a short time later when they pulled up to the grocery store.

"Why don't you just leave baby Wyatt here with me while you run in and get what we're going to need for tonight?" Ruby offered.

Maggie smiled and rushed inside. For the second time in a week, she strolled through aisles and purchased things for the baby.

"I thought about a baby bed for the night," she said when she returned to the car. "Aunt Marjorie used to tell a story about how my great-grandmother put her babies in a dresser drawer. She had them so close together she ran out of room for the newest one."

Ruby laughed. "My grandmother did the same thing," she said. "I guess little Wyatt will spend his first night in his grandma's bureau drawers."

"Wyatt Sharpe," Maggie said aloud. She glanced in her rearview mirror at the small car seat strapped in her back seat. "It rolls right off the tongue, doesn't it?"

"Sure does," Ruby agreed. "Let's get him home and fed. I'm going to stick around and help you tonight."

CHAPTER SIXTEEN

It was five in the morning when Ruby and Maggie, both sleep-deprived with baby Wyatt in tow, arrived at the donut shop the next day. They agreed to take turns tending to him in the office while attending to business as usual for the day.

Maggie proposed the idea of using the mini donut machines in the food truck for daily specials while Wyatt was in her care. As soon as the five and dime opened downtown she intended to send Myra after a portable baby bed.

Orson was the first to hear the baby fussing in the office. "What is going on?" he demanded, looking warily toward the office door. "Please don't tell me that we're opening a daycare here."

"No one is opening any daycare here, Orson," Maggie said. "But my grandson has been placed in my care for the time being. And I have a business to run," Maggie said. "So as long as he's with me, he'll be here."

Orson's eyes widened. "Your grandbaby is here?" He moved quietly to the office door for a peek. "I don't want to wake him up. I just want a quick look."

Maggie was stunned by the change in his demeanor. She expected a grumpy, frustrated old man. What she got instead was a sweet, gently surprised friend.

"He's so adorable," Orson whispered. "I can't believe how sweet he is."

"We're taking turns with him," she said.

"Count me in the rotation," he said. "I can hold him while I'm on my breaks. He can sit with me and the other old men."

Wyatt woke up just before the doors opened for the day. Maggie rushed into the office with a freshly made bottle in her hand. She shut the door and laid a blanket over her desk to change him. Carefully she removed him from the car seat and cuddled him against her chest. "Good morning, baby boy," she whispered.

After a quick change, she settled into the office chair to feed him. The formula disappeared quickly. He burped easily and then laid quietly in her arms, wide awake and gazing around the room. Ruby pushed the door open slightly and watched. "Looks like our little man has a healthy appetite," she said.

"That he does," Maggie replied. She didn't take her eyes off of him as she spoke.

"Myra has gone after a bed," Ruby continued. "Larry down at the five and dime said that he would open up the store an hour early for her, but you owe him a dozen donuts sometime next week."

"Done," Maggie said quietly. "What made him agree to open up for us?"

"I think Brett must have talked to him because he called me on my cell phone a little while ago and said that he heard it through the grapevine that we needed a baby bed," Ruby said. "Larry is my neighbor. He has a farm just south of mine."

"I wonder if we are going to hear anything more about the case," Maggie said. She looked down at Wyatt who was cooing softly in her arms. "The best news I could get today would be that my son was released from jail, free to come and meet his son."

"Maggie, you know that there is a possibility," Ruby said. She stopped short of reminding Maggie that the baby might not be her son's flesh and blood.

"I am very aware of the possibilities," Maggie said. "But it doesn't matter. That is a bridge we will cross when we come to it."

"Would you like a quick break? I can hold him," Ruby offered. Maggie smiled and stood up and placed the baby gingerly in her arms.

"I'll be right back," she said. She ran straight for the employee restroom in the kitchen and grabbed a water bottle from the stash in the cooler on her way back. When she returned, the baby had fallen back to sleep. "I guess we can lay him in the car seat again, at least until Myra returns with the bed."

Maggie sat and watched baby Wyatt sleep for as long as she could.

Orson announced that it was his turn to feed Wyatt during the mid-morning lull in business. He sat with the other old-timers at their table near the front windows of the donut shop. Maggie stole glances at him as often as she could get away with.

Orson held the little one like he was his grandson. Myra went out of her way to stop in and look at him between tasks.

"It wouldn't be so bad, would it?" Ruby asked Maggie. They stood together behind the display case in the front. Maggie had just replaced an empty tray with a fresh batch of cinnamon scones.

"What? Raising Wyatt?"

Ruby shrugged. "Raising him, at least part of the time," she said. "This would definitely be a group project."

"I think you're right about that," Maggie said.

Maggie bent down and began moving donuts around in the display case, both to free up near-empty trays and get a good count for what she needed to plan for the rest of the day.

While her head was still in the case, Ruby tapped her vigorously on her shoulder. "Maggie," she said. "Brett just pulled up, and he isn't alone."

Maggie rose and gazed out of the window to the parking lot. Brett was out there parked about three spaces from the front door. Brooks exited the front passenger side followed by someone else in the back.

Her heart believed it before her head did. She wiped her hands on the front of her apron and smoothed down her shirt.

"It's him." She moved around Ruby and headed for the front. Brooks paused and held the door open. Bradley walked slowly inside the donut shop. His blond hair was slightly disheveled, and he needed a good shave, but overall, he appeared no worse for wear.

He smiled broadly. "Mom," he said and rushed toward her. He caught her in a strong embrace. "I don't think I have ever been more excited to smell fresh donuts in my life."

Maggie pushed back gently and looked up at her son. "How did you get out?" she asked.

"I'm going to let the police chief explain all of that," he said. "Right now, I want to get a hold of my little boy."

Orson stood up and walked over to where they stood. He gently laid the baby in Bradley's arms and stepped back.

"Hello there, little man," Bradley cooed. "I don't even know your name."

"I heard you liked Wyatt." Maggie beamed. "He didn't have a name when they called me to the police station, so I picked that one for now based on what you told me before."

Bradley settled the baby in the crook of his arm. "She hadn't chosen a name?" Maggie shook her head. "It's definitely Wyatt. He looks like a Wyatt, doesn't he?" He smiled and bent over to kiss the little boy on the top of his head.

"Let's go over here," Ruby suggested. Maggie noticed her for the first time since Brett pulled up. She led them to the far side of the donut shop where the booths lined the side of the counter. "Brett, can you please fill us in on what is happening?"

Brett took a seat in the booth. "As you know, Cynthia was arrested along with Pete Deluca after a disturbance at Dogwood House."

"Have they been charged?" Maggie asked.

"Deluca has been charged with the murder of J.J. McCoy," Brett said. "His prints match those on your son's dog tags. That's why he sat for so long without formal charges. Bradley's prints were not found in McCoy's vehicle."

"Why, though?" Ruby asked. "What was the motive?"

"I'll let Officer Brooks explain," he said. "He was a big part of figuring things out."

"Truthfully, it was all Maggie. I think we need to consult with her on things from now on." He winked at Brett who had immediately rolled his eyes. "We looked a little further into those social media posts you found with all four, McCoy, Cynthia, and Deluca, and Boone. After a short conversation with the naval attorney, it didn't take long to find a link."

"They were dating... Wait, *were* right? Not are? Please tell me Cynthia was not seeing my son and Pete at the same time."

"They had been in a relationship in the past," Brooks replied. "And like you said, Pete is not military after all. He was best friends with Cynthia's brother, Cal."

"And how does he fit into all of this? Why was he looking around for my son and why was he in my house? I've heard good stories about that boy, and I don't want to believe that someone who my son thought was a true friend was anything but."

"All three guys are best friends. But Cal knew that both J.J. and Pete were known for causing trouble so when he heard about J.J.'s death, he came here to try to help. He thought his sister was maybe staying at your house which is why he was there. He came to warn all of you, but it didn't go as planned. He has apologized profusely for scaring you and would love to talk with you before he leaves."

"So, Pete got mad Bradley is married to his old girlfriend? But what does that have to do with J.J.?" Maggie asked, no longer concerned with the man who had been in her house.

"Pete found out that his relationship with Cynthia was officially over, despite how many times she'd told him."

"And he somehow stole my son's dog tags and attempted to frame him for murder?"

"On the nose. I'm telling you, Brett. Your girl has a real knack for this." Brooks laughed. "Pete believed that J.J. was the one to introduce Bradley and Cynthia. He apparently was all about their relationship and felt your son was better suited for Cynthia and Pete didn't like that."

"Well, what she doesn't know is that Cynthia went with Deluca to meet McCoy the night he was killed."

"You mentioned that earlier." She smirked. "Does that mean she was involved in the murder?" Maggie asked.

"The truth is, we aren't quite sure just what level of involvement Cynthia had with the murder. We believe she was present, but don't have many details or anything solid to prove that yet. Another thing we don't know is whether she was a participant or a victim herself."

"Cynthia is not talking to anyone about her involvement," Brooks added. "She started off asking for an attorney. She has denied any request to contact her family. I'm not sure what is going on with her, but she is clearly not going to make things easy."

"Has she said anything about… well, anything?" Ruby asked.

"Only that she is so sorry for everything she has put Bradley through," Brooks said gently. "She isn't saying much, but she did insist that she cared about him. She asked one of the deputies at the jail to set up a meeting with a social worker. She wants to talk about signing her rights over to Bradley."

At last, Bradley, who had been close enough to hear everything, spoke, "I knew she had been seeing Pete before we met, but she told me they'd broken up. Cynthia and I, we really hit it off when we met. It was like something out of a romance movie."

"But Bradley," Maggie said. "Are you worried at all about the timing of the birth? What do you think about her signing her rights over?"

Bradley sighed and kissed Wyatt again. He raised his eyes to meet his mother's, and then looked around at the other faces gathered close by. "I am only going to address this once, so listen closely," he said. "By law, since I was married to Cynthia when Wyatt was born, my name goes on the birth certificate. Already, three people have asked me about a paternity test, and I will tell you as I told them. I don't ever want to hear another question about it. The timing could be right, and I trust that she was honest with me because of the connection we had. She might have done bad things, but we all have. Somehow, Cynthia and I will figure out our future."

"Good man," Orson said and rubbed Bradley's shoulder.

Bradley raised the baby to his cheek. "This is my son. He will always be my son, and nobody is going to question that," he continued. "My lawyer secured emergency leave for me and will work to get three more weeks of parental leave after that. I assumed that we could stay with you for now, Mom, if that's okay?"

"Of course," Maggie smiled. She leaned up to kiss her son and grandson on their cheeks. "Will you remain in the Navy then?"

Bradley settled the baby back in his arms and nodded. "Right now, that is the plan," he said. "I think I can make a much better life for the two of us that way. I don't have to remain at sea forever."

Maggie reached for the baby and cradled him in her arms. "Sounds to me that you and your daddy were both caught up in someone else's mess, little one," she said.

"You can say that again, Mom," Bradley said. "But look what we got out of this mess."

"I see an entire week of blueberry donuts celebrating this little boy's birth," Ruby said.

"A week? Rookie," Orson snorted. "I think we need an entirely new line of treats named after Baby Wyatt. Pay attention, Bradley, you'll find out quickly who's the brains of the outfit around here."

AUTHOR'S NOTE

I'd love to hear your thoughts on my books, the story-lines, and anything else that you'd like to comment on —reader feedback is very important to me. My contact information, along with some other helpful links, is listed on the next page. If you'd like to be on my list of "folks to contact" with updates, release and sales notifications, etc.... just shoot me an email and let me know. Thanks for reading!

Also...

... if you're looking for more great reads, Summer Prescott Books publishes several popular series by outstanding Cozy Mystery authors.

CONTACT SUMMER PRESCOTT BOOKS PUBLISHING

Blog and Book Catalog: http://summerprescottbooks.com

Email: summer.prescott.cozies@gmail.com

And…be sure to check out the Summer Prescott Cozy Mysteries fan page and Summer Prescott Books Publishing Page on Facebook – let's be friends!

To sign up for our fun and exciting newsletter, which will give you opportunities to win prizes and swag, enter contests, and be the first to know about New Releases, click here: http://summerprescottbooks.com

Made in United States
North Haven, CT
23 February 2022

16421717R00078